At the Closing of th

ONE

College seemed to be about time. Natalie was figuring out how to shoehorn hobbies and activities she wanted to try in between classes and social engagements, and if possible, wedge in some time to sleep and eat. It was a balancing act, which was new to her, just as living in a rental house and sharing a kitchen with someone else was new. Everything had to be slotted in or not accomplished, yet

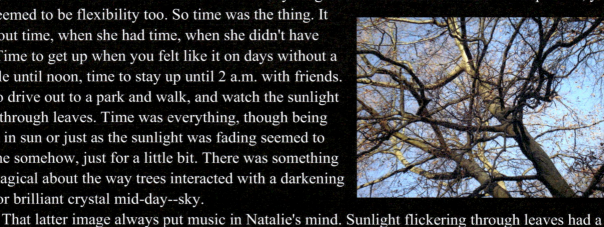

there seemed to be flexibility too. So time was the thing. It was about time, when she had time, when she didn't have time. Time to get up when you felt like it on days without a schedule until noon, time to stay up until 2 a.m. with friends. Time to drive out to a park and walk, and watch the sunlight flicker through leaves. Time was everything, though being outside in sun or just as the sunlight was fading seemed to halt time somehow, just for a little bit. There was something truly magical about the way trees interacted with a darkening blue --or brilliant crystal mid-day--sky.

That latter image always put music in Natalie's mind. Sunlight flickering through leaves had a flavor to it and a calming property that made her relax and feel like there was magic all around despite the prosaic needs of full-time school, bills and laundry, social interactions and roommate issues. The way a slight breeze could move a summer wind around through the trees with a quiet shushing voice, dappling the ground with shadows was magical. Probably this came from an inherited interest in folklore and the Old Ways, and just plain love of music; Natalie knew a lot about plants, not just to name them on walks but also medicinal properties, or traditional magical uses. And there were songs about nearly all of that which her mother knew, so she knew. That was how it all started.

It had been at one of the first parties of the quarter and Natalie was standing with a friend she barely knew near the kitchenette holding a room-temperature glass just tapped from a keg of beer that

she didn't even like (and was technically illegal for her to have) and rambling with Joann about whatever because it was so noisy in this antique rental living room that she was sure no one could hear them farther than about 12" away. The green shag carpet and 1970s vintage fabric hangings on the stained pale-yellow walls barely muffled the roar of first-years laughing, acting up and generally trying to make themselves heard and noticed amid a sea of same. It turned out Joann, call me Jo, had a mother who worked at an arboretum. Natalie knew plants too, so the talk veered into

the language of flowers, which was both botanical and historic. Victorians in particular used to use flowers to indicate messages without resorting to words. It was apparently a very long catalog, and highly detailed.

"For instance," Joann said, " Geranium can mean anything from melancholy to comfort depending what color it is."

Natalie grimaced a smile,

"I just know the basics. White roses for purity, red for love."

Joann nodded,

"But it's so fussy." This was both a laughed complaint and an expression of the sort of passionate interest Nat had noticed in all her class mates. It seemed like people in this environment found something they liked then got rabid about it and absorbed way more information than anyone really was likely to ever need, unless they were mastering in the subject. Jo might be thinking that way about floral language because she started listing. "A burgundy rose is unconscious love but a dark red is bashfulness, while a red and white one is unity and cabbage roses or the stage of the bloom change it again."

"How did anyone remember all that?" Natalie glanced around the room where the sound of conversation buzzed at deafening levels and saw at least five other sets of people talking pretty much exactly as she and Jo were talking. Amid that, some people were just drifting around with faint grins while others were drunkenly performing, as on a stage. Eighteen to twenty-two was a crazy time.

Joann gulped some forbidden beer so she could clear her mouth to answer,

"They just did. Like how did guys in the 18th century know what a girl was saying just by how she was holding her fan?"

Natalie nodded, suspecting that bit of information might have come from movies rather than books but determined to contribute if they were going to get detailed, said,

"I know more about the magical uses of plants than the language of flowers."

"Name one," Jo challenged, game.

"Vervain is an herb used to protect against evil. For another, theyt say belladonna was used in flying ointment that witches made with fat, usually from some horrible source like hanged men..."

"...like a hand of glory," Jo inserted with ghoulish delight, then added, "That stuff is really toxic."

Natalie grinned and nodded,

"That's how it made them fly. Get that and other poisons in an open wound or cut and you had hallucinations. Of course, the black color of the berries probably helped. How about that mushroom called Dead Man's Fingers?"

One of the people wandering through in search of the next drink or conversation overheard this and he said,

"Or mandrake, of course, thank you Harry Potter."

Natalie wasn't sure if he was ribbing them because they were clearly first-years or not. He was obviously at least 21 and tall, reasonably attractive. It helped that he was relaxed and calm, not one of the people trying desperately to be entertaining. Natalie, somewhat intimidated by an Older Guy, spoke up by way of self-defense.

"Thank you, Bible, you mean. It's in Genesis."

The man laughed.

"Nice come-back. You know a lot about this stuff, both of you."

He included Jo in the glance and Natalie liked him for it. He wasn't being creepy or trying to pick one of them up, at least not yet, and he wasn't singling one of them out. Of course, that might just be a way of not scaring off the young things; if he made up to the wing man, he had a better chance with the target and he must know that, yet it didn't seem premeditated or predatory.

Joann didn't show any indication that she was thinking as hard about all this as Natalie was, and just said,

"We're plant geeks."

"Going in for botany then?"

Jo shrugged but Natalie said,

"Not just. Folklore is more interesting."

"You're majoring in folklore?"

"I'm not majoring in anything yet," was the obvious reply. She set her beer down on the table next to her, deciding she was done with it and the gesture changed the subject.

"Don't like it?" He sipped his and almost unconsciously Jo sipped hers. Natalie just said,

"Not really. Too sour. I'm Natalie, this is Jo."

"Matt."

"Nice to meet you Matt."

"Nice to meet you. Hey, are you girls interested in music?"

Aha, Natalie thought, here is the pickup line.

"I play guitar but I can't seem to find enough people who want to collaborate on something other than Top 40 and hard rock. I like folk or classical guitar better. Just looking for people who like to play."

Natalie glanced at Jo who was just watching Matt steadily but not sharply. She looked like she was humming under her breath and not really paying attention. Nat said,

"I have a keyboard but I haven't got a lot of time for a band." Then she added, "I know a lot of folk songs, anyway."

"Any spooky ones?" Joann said it while moving to the thumping of the stereo base. She almost shouted it because of the noise in the room, but like the rest of the discussion, it didn't travel very far for the same reason. When the two looked at her, she added, "Halloween coming up."

Matt grinned,

"Sure, why not? There are plenty creepy folk songs." Then to Natalie in regard to time for a band, he said, "How about just some jam sessions? Meet me in the Student Union Hall Friday afternoon and let's see what happens. Both of you come." The last was said with a lift of the beer and didn't seem at all like he was singling Natalie out. His eyes sort of did that, but then again, Jo wasn't really giving Matt her attention and that might be what Nat was seeing. Natalie hesitated, wondering if she was asking for trouble but when she glanced at Jo and got a disinterested nod implying Joann would come along with her, she said,

"Okay, see you then."

There was one other person in the SU when Nat and Jo walked in after their last classes Friday.

The day had gone from foggy half overcast in the morning to some rain sprinkles, to a glorious golden sun-washed afternoon, still damp and slightly cool but with enough humidity to signal a warmer day tomorrow and a long weekend of seeing and doing new things, rubbing interests against other people's to see what sparked a connection, and rushing to finish homework on Sunday night. Right now, the sunlight had a dusty sparkling look as it filtered into the dirty windows of the lobby, illuminating old industrial carpet woven with the University's logo. The logo was faded down the middle where feet had walked for decades and the door squeaked, announcing their arrival. Through the open door to the auditorium, two faces could be seen glancing up from the distant stage. One was Matt, the other a girl about his age.

Natalie was a little disappointed to see the girl, though she wasn't sure why. It wasn't like she'd hoped Matt would ask her out but somehow seeing an older woman (20 or 21, so no old, just older than the newcomers) as part of the proposed band practice changed the dynamic. Probably because it made her feel like a kid among adults, she responded to the challenge, imagined or not, with the same sort of perspective she had when kids back in high school had managed to make her feel inferior: she turned on her cultivated detachment and walked straight down the aisle with Jo in train, like she had been here many times. She hadn't, of course. The Student Union building was generations old but a little out of use in an age of pandemics and social media so she'd been in the main lobby once while matriculating, and hadn't been in since.

The auditorium looked old, like a theater from the 1920s but not fancy like commercial spaces. It had the feeling of an old beat-up vaudeville road house with wooden seats vestigially padded in worn wine-red wool and a proscenium arch with a simple lintel design. The side drapes looked moth-eaten and the stage back was a flat made of scuffed old plywood that had been painted matte black probably when Natalie was still in preschool. On this unimpressive stage, Matt and the other girl were setting up a microphone and amp. Matt wore a guitar slung around his back as he crouched, tinkering with the equipment. The girl was dealing with the mic stand in a way that implied practice, which told Natalie she was probably a singer. That was as well: Natalie had an okay voice but she had no wish to be a lead. Jo probably did, though, and as they reached the orchestra pit, which was mostly just a flat space without seats, not large, Jo whispered into Nat's ear,

"Who is she?"

Natalie thought she could hear some annoyance in there so maybe Jo had hoped to be the lead singer-- or possibly she wanted to date Matt--but Natalie ignored it all and called up,

"Hi."

Matt looked down and smiled at them both,

"I saw you but I can't get this thing to sync," he explained, as if they'd noticed and cared that he hadn't reacted to their arrival.

Again, maybe Jo had cared but Natalie just smiled and started to the side steps,

"I don't have my keyboard here yet." Her feet sounded loud on the stage boards. She went right to the girl and said, "Hi, I'm Natalie, this is Joann."

The girl clipped the microphone into the stand and turned. Her expression was open but also measuring as she introduced herself,

"Karla. Do you sing?"

It was such an echo to what Nat had been thinking that she hesitated, but Joann said,

"Pretty good. Natalie does awesome harmony."

"If I know the song," Natalie tempered instantly, irritated. Joann hadn't let her speak for herself, a first, though admittedly she'd known the girl for a month but it was sort of like Jo was already competing with Karla. There had been a sort of sense of one-upmanship in her tone.

Thankfully Karla either didn't notice or didn't care.

"Great. What songs do you know that are simple enough we can try them today?"

By then, Matt had got his amp working and was running some chords. After bouncing some ideas of popular songs around, they settled on the American folksong *Poor Wayfaring Stranger* and tried it out.

Having three girls on one mic was awkward so they paused to get another plugged in for Natalie, and the next few runs they did, Karla and Jo alternated as lead singer. It was interesting. The amplified music and voice traveled out into the empty theater and filled it, washing back and forth from wall to wall, and over the seats without anything to muffle it and it made Natalie hyper aware of her own voice but after a little nervousness, she was able to forget about it and try different things. She did wish she had her keyboard though. She was still unsure enough of herself that she didn't quite know what to do with her hands.

They paused after running the song three times all the way through, and in the quiet that suddenly seemed strong with the ceasing of the music, Jo made a comment about folk songs.

"We talked about doing witch music," she said, with a slight tone Natalie read as partial respect for Karla's vocals and partial ongoing competition for attention.

"Did we?" Matt sounded surprised but stopped tuning and turned to look at her with his full attention.

Natalie again found herself temporizing,

"Jo and I did. I think all the three of us discussed was folk songs." She smiled at Jo to soften what probably sounded like a correction. "It's just Jo and I like the spooky ones best."

Matt shrugged, glanced at Karla and strummed a chord that vibrated out into the space,

"Fine by me. Know any spooky folk songs, Karl?"

The older girl was trying to find another microphone in the mess of gear she had apparently found backstage, given the age of the case and the snarl of the cords. She said rather absently,

"In a haunted theater?"

Natalie shot her a sharp glance. Was she joking? It was hard to tell. Joann just asked for details.

"Is it haunted? How?"

Karla stood up with an antique-looking mic in her hand and blew hair out of her eyes,

"Huh? Oh. Something about a student fell from the grid and died onstage in the 1960s or something."

Matt gave her a half-squint that looked derisive or like he was trying to discourage the

conversation. Karla saw it but said, "She asked."

Natalie was glad she didn't say "they asked", which would've lumped her with Jo as the inquisitive little kid, because Karla's tone had had an edge that implied for the first time that she felt some aggressiveness from Joann. Feeling that familiar but always uncomfortable shift of interest from one new friend to another that you felt you might be closer to in opinions, Natalie said,

"I'm interested too but for now can we just pick a song? I have a ton of homework to do this weekend and I want to get started so I can actually enjoy the weather."

She was aware she sounded like her mother but relieved that the older kids seemed pleased by the digression. Matt smiled at her a little ironically and said,

"So do I. Name a few of your spooky songs."

Natalie named a handful of Child's collected ballads but they didn't know them. Yet. Matt and Karla both said they were fast on picking up new songs if they could hear them, so Natalie said she'd find recordings or at least sheet music with lyrics and bring them next time. Until then, what should they try?

"How about *Scarborough Fair*?" Matt rang a string of notes rapidly, like water falling in crystals.

"I only know the Simon and Garfunkel," Natalie warned.

"Works. Has good harmonies," said Karla casually, almost visibly moving them on without reference to Joann, but she did set up the third mic. Natalie, in the interests of preventing a skirmish, took it. It was farthest from center stage and incidentally Matt who said with a smile directed at both girls,

"That one has herbs in it so it's right up your alley, botany girls."

The sun was going down by the time they left the theater, Matt locking the place up behind them and pushing the key through a mail slot on the front door while juggling his gear. What had been a golden afternoon had vanished into a cold autumn night and there was a hint of rain in the air, and a stiff breeze pushing the trees around beneath the streetlights, which were beginning to cast moving shadows like skeletal arms all over the concrete. Leaves brushed past on the wind and Natalie thought about the wiccan aspects of the song they'd just done. It had a lot more impact when you were walking around outside at night. Karla had a car, admittedly a small beater that looked like someone had sat on a gumdrop then spray-painted it red. It was only just big enough to fit her gear and Matt's and she jokingly, but with a straight face, informed him she was giving his gear a ride, not him. The tone had a note of tradition and Matt grinned. It looked like they'd been friends a long time and Natalie at least was not sure if that was better or worse than boyfriend-girlfriend, as it meant Matt was once more possibly available. Joann didn't really notice any of the interchange. She was thinking, so not talkative. Natalie walked back with her to the dorms where Jo lived, and just past which was the south

border of campus beyond which was the neighborhood where Natalie rented a room in a house.

It was an old house. Given the darkness and the mood, it didn't look very welcoming as she went in the side with her key. The light over the door flickered: it did that a lot. Even in the month she'd been here, that bulb didn't seem to last at all. It made the side entrance even more eerie and she hurried inside to a landing that led to a short flight of red steps: like many single-family homes in a college town, it'd been

subdivided into two units and the division had played merry hell with the original functional architecture. This side door had originally led only to the basement, and that staircase stretched off to the side of the landing she passed, gaping darkly and feeling like someone was standing at the bottom of the steps in the dark, watching. It always felt like that but tonight it felt like it more intensely and she did not linger getting the inside kitchen door open. Once her feet struck linoleum, she flicked on the kitchen light to

alleviate some of the spooks she'd just given herself. Old houses made it so easy to imagine yourself into the heebie jeebies. With the light on, a good part of the creeps receded, though the place felt too quiet without her roommate. Still, the worn yellowing floor pattern and the weird woodwork with fourteen layers and fifty years of paint on it were comforting. Somehow it seemed like every old rental in town had that sort of woodwork: probably once handmade and beautiful, it had all received so many layers of paint, usually topped by pale yellow, that the place had a look of having been carved out of rancid butter. It made her smile and she got out her books on the kitchen table, put on a tea kettle for cocoa and settled in for some studying.

At home, she'd had a shed in the back yard that her Dad had set up for her own private study use, to keep the noise and energy of her siblings Angela and Brad at bay while she needed to concentrate. Here, tonight at least, the silence of the house had the opposite effect of that isolated bubble of focus. She seemed to not be able to keep her attention from expanding to fill the whole floor (the upstairs being rented by people who were out of town right now, she didn't include that in her personal space). The stairs to the basement were the most obvious, even way over there and a locked door away. She made every attempt to read the source material on her base class in English composition that every first-year had to take to remind them of everything they'd forgotten from grade school, but the stairs were so huge in her awareness that eventually she gave up and went to bed. Making damn sure to close her bedroom door. She didn't get much sleep though, until her roommate, Peg, came in about midnight. Natalie sighed with relief. Somehow not being alone in the house helped her feel less vulnerable. Not that Peg would do anything but probably laugh if she mentioned the whole thing. Drat the ghost stories anyway. Karla must have been trying to scare the children. Well, Natalie had been around ghosts before. She was determined it wasn't going to get to her. She wouldn't let it.

TWO

The music sessions became a regular event, though after the second, Joann suddenly 'discovered' that she was too busy to participate anymore. Natalie was a little sorry to see her go but at the same time, didn't take it personally. Mom and Dad had both talked about how early college friendships were mostly shallow, purely social contacts that sifted out and drifted away as time went on. It was the one or two really close friendships one made that lasted into later life. Mom still kept in touch with two or three of her old college friends and Dad still got together with a man he'd known in high school. This was all normal and you tried not to feel hurt when people snubbed you or just stopped coming around. It was still partly high school, Mom had pointed out. People didn't change that fast, even in the permissive and expanding atmosphere of collegiate endeavor.

This didn't necessarily include romances, of course, though Natalie was still not ready to start looking at the guys she met as potential partners. She did admit privately that Matt was sort of super attractive, with dark hair that he usually didn't comb but which managed to look sexy without it looking dirty, and the deft talent he had when he played guitar. On the other hand, he could be really forgetful or distracted and it didn't lead Nat to assume she had a special place in this mind when he would sometimes walk by her on campus without even apparently seeing her. That had bothered her at first until once, he did it with Karla in tow and Karla had made a face at his back and greeted Natalie, which told Nat it was not her at all but just his way. That she could live with. It also helped her distance her feelings a little. Karla was proving to be a neat friend, not too close, still a bit adult so feeling ahead of Nat, but not condescending at any point. Sometimes Nat thought Karla was watching her closely to make sure she didn't get a crush on Matt or his friends, who occasionally sat in on the music. That was fine. Natalie had the firm intention to not disappoint her and so far, was so busy outside the jam sessions that it hadn't been an issue. Most of her days were consumed by school work and classes anyway, which kept her firmly in her own age-level, not withstanding occasional older students that were coming back to college after their kids had left home. One of her classmates in social anthropology was 75 and because of his enthusiasm for the topcs, he

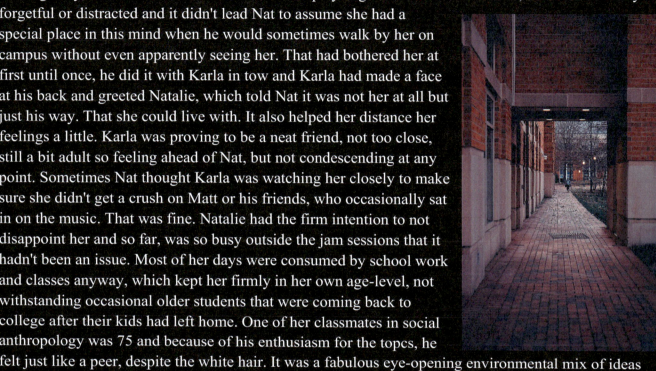

felt just like a peer, despite the white hair. It was a fabulous eye-opening environmental mix of ideas and people. Natalie could see why sometimes her parents talked about college with affection and nostalgia even while admitting the degree didn't help realistically with the current job market.

One of the aforementioned of Matt's friends who sat in a few times eventually became a regular. He had introduced himself as Thranduil, his LARP Elven name, but his real name was Terry. The latter had been told to Natalie by Karla, sotto voce as an aside, which echoed Natalie's opinion about the choice. The name had struck even Natalie, still absorbing alternative cultures at this stage in her first year, as silly. For your character in a role game, sure. Asking people to call you that seemed vaguely desperate. Then again, this guy had shown up with an actual Roman gladius sword strapped to his back; it wasn't a short sword. He'd been adamant and verbose about that point. Natalie had heard about half, then heard "SCA" and tuned out, nodding occasionally with a faint smile on. At least he had taken the sword off to play the guitar he was carrying. And she had to admit he was talented, and the addition of a second guitar helped fill out the sound greatly. He also had a tin whistle, which he almost apologized for because it was not a proper flute. Karla told him penny whistles were extremely common in folk music because of the Irish tradition and American itinerant history. Thranduil made a half scowl, which implied he was way more interested in mythic pasts than real ones. Natalie managed to pour oil on the waters by mentioning that the original version of *Scarborough Fair*, which they had been practicing, was a version of a Child ballad called *The Elfin Knight* and was numbered 2 which implied it was collected very early. That seemed to help and they got back to the simple pleasure of making music, instead of arguing.

The selection of what they wanted to play came up a few weeks in, and they all came to the practice space with ideas. Natalie showed a sheaf of Child's ballads but pointed out how many were either dialectically difficult, super long or about distasteful subjects like incest and rape. She flatly refused to do sexual ones or child murder but had brought songs featuring ghosts, demons, fairies and witches. Karla thumbed through them first since she was the one who was going to have to learn the lyrics from scratch and said she was pretty sure she could American-ize them to some degree so she'd have a go. Thranduil's contributions were primarily Lord of the Rings, of course, but also several fantasy classics, including *The Lady of Shallot* which Natalie knew from a modern recording. Karla skimmed it, then handed it to Matt who made a face over the lyrical construction. Thranduil said, rather defensively,

"It's better with music."

Natalie, who couldn't agree more, found the Loreena McKennit arrangement on her cell phone while the others talked various options, and played it out loud for them. The artist's choices were almost flawless for the song and while her phone made it sound tinny, the web of glittering magic woven by the wordplay when set to a flowing melody was undeniable. She could almost see the golden fields, the river winding down to Camelot, the storm clouds gathering, the boat on the water at dusk with its glowing faint white figure lying prone and singing her holy carol.

She didn't have to say anything about it; though it was a long piece, they listened to it uninterrupted. Then Matt said,

"Okay. We'll put it on the maybe list. But it's really long."

Karla, with papers in her hands, said,

"Most of the Child's are longer. We can edit for time."

Having proven that music can make anything sound amazing, Natalie and Thranduil just glanced at each other and then got back to the things Matt had brought (mostly American folk based on UK, none of it ghostly though some of it supernaturally tinted). Karla had only mentioned a few bands she liked and had not brought specific suggestions.

The haunting thing came up again when Thranduil started commenting on the sound in the empty space, then segued into trying to spook the girls by talking about the theater legend. They had been discussing songs that harked

to Lord of the Rings, suggested by Thranduil of course. The old English tunes had given way to Led Zepplin just for fun, in this case *Kashmir*, and in the break between songs, Thranduil had repeated a verse:

Oh, father of the four winds fill my sails;
Cross the sea of years
With no provision but an open face
Along the straits of fear

He paused as if to let the words settle in, a slight echo coming back from the empty seats because of the stage-cast voice he'd used to broadcast the line as if it were a poem. Then he turned to Natalie and said to her directly, "The straits of fear. You know this theater is haunted, right?"

The song had been pure summer sunshine and grassy hills of imagination, but when Thranduil started to speak, the gray rain outside seemed to close back in and make the theater lights dim. Natalie said calmly,
"I heard something like that." Her tone didn't encourage him to elaborate and she tinkered with her keyboard settings to see if she could get a heavier sound out of it. The song really needed a hard stomping base-end and drums to work.
Thranduil grinned.
"A student threw herself off the balcony because her boyfriend cheated. She was about your age."
Nat raised her head and looked right at him, letting him see her unsmiling, unimpressed expression and Karla, who had done an amazing job singing the main line of *Kashmir* like one of the Wilson sisters from Heart, said,
"When you say stupid things, you look more like Hugo Weaving than Orlando Bloom." Since this was the old guy, not the young hottie (well, back then. The movies were so old now), it served to take some of the wind out of Thranduil and he looked irritated, brows drawing down and for the moment, more petulant child than glamorous knight errant:
"The books, not the movies," he said. Then he stated, "Matt told me. " He turned to the other man, "You hear noises when you're alone like footsteps and crying. You were totally freaked out."
Matt didn't look freaked out but his eyes were flat which indicated he wasn't happy with either the levity about ghosts or the direct accusation. His expression was almost a dare that Thranduil make fun of him. As for direct comment, he made none, only saying blandly,
"It sounds so much better with a full drum kit."

It was starting to rain again as they left and this time, they were leaving the amps locked in a back room, so Matt was riding home. This was the day Natalie learned he rode a motorcycle, which was why he got rides with Karla when the amps had to be moved. With just the guitar, he could wear it across his back and ride. The parallel between Matt on an iron horse with his guitar on looking casual and practiced like this was no big deal and Thranduil's Roman sword slung across his back as he strode off into the rain was obvious and made the last song feel more immediate. Somehow the sword still looked affected, while the motorcyclist looked like something half overshadowed by Tennyson poetry and the false romance of the Knights of the Round Table in denim and leather, but Natalie had started reading Lord of the Rings: The Fellowship to see what kind of literature inspired Thranduil's level of devotion and she could see how it  translated to real life, at least in the artistic permissiveness of college towns. The books were completely immersive and made you want to be part of the world. But the name Thranduil was still a bit silly, she thought.

On a downside, she was pretty sure the fantasy novel was influencing her imagination heavily, because when she got home in the dark, the thing on the basement stairs seemed even more present than usual and it was definitely watching as she shot through the double doors, being absolutely sure to lock the inside door against the staircase. Silly. Silly to be spooked at all but sometimes you couldn't help it and with barrow wights and Nazgul on her mind, she went to bed, glad that Peg was home tonight. She could hear the faint trickle of radio music as Peg studied in the living room, and it added a layer of comfort to not be alone.

Natalie, like any teenager, was very emotionally involved with music and the way a song could speak of your own feelings or lift you above the normal, everyday problems was a kind of magic of its own. One of Thranduil's pieces that he'd shared was an instrumental called *The Ships of the Immortals* by a new age band called Gandalf. The music was simple so easy to learn and so lovely and drifting and immersive, that she understood better why Thranduil was wearing that sword. They had tried it with Matt's guitar at its most river-like and Thranduil's penny whistle. The keyboard added a nice layer and both girls just hummed, since there were no lyrics but it had worked very nicely and woven almost a spell. It felt like they were standing on the deck of a graceful wooden ship decorated with Elven carvings and drifting gently along the rivers of Rivendell like a swan in a lake. The tune had a beauty and the lack of lyrics kept it from seeming pretentious. It was also easily translated to their simple means and that resonated: for all those bands that weren't high-tech with expensive production values but just basic talent and time, for every time Natalie had felt somewhere in her head that "I could do that", that opened a door. Natalie felt like she was standing at that door, and it fed back to her from late high school, where the creation of yourself by social interactions at parties, clubs, concerts, had that possibility inherent. You could do that. You may or may not *want* to because it was a ton of hard work for little payback and no certain future but to make music with others because you wanted to make a sound that spoke your emotions and opinions, that was something. It was a thing worth experimenting with and college was if nothing else about experimenting. As her dad used to say, throw it all at the wall and see what sticks. So far this was sticking. At least it was sticking between classes.

The evenings and weekends were when it stuck best. As the day went down, then the magic started. It was like the dim unseen possibility that had been behind the curtain during a day of stress and business trying to get work done while tired and honestly overwhelmed came back into focus and filled the entire world even as the sun slowed, stalled, sank. Then the cool blues of dusk and darkness were absolutely wide open with what could be and with whatever nebulous power it was that allowed young people to make it that. Mom had said that ability faded as you aged and while it never vanished completely if you were creative, it definitely became much harder to tap. Natalie, from here in the encompassing warmth of the creative, didn't see how that could be though she knew Mom was almost always right. It just didn't seem like the pool of magic could be drained. With all four of the band feeding into it several times a week and with the constant daily influx of ideas and influences, new people and new ideas, it was more like it wouldn't shut up. But it was wonderful even if she never seemed to get enough sleep.

Natalie was well aware that scent had the ability to bring back in sharp focus an entire mood or situation. She physically remembered standing in a friend's bedroom as a child whenever she smelled a big white floral perfume, because that friend's grandmother had given her a bottle of gardenia cologne, but she more firmly believed that music had the ability to conjure up not only the past but also to weave futures. Music floated the mind and touched the soul. It came from both. Who doesn't have a song list of artists that got them through the high school years, or vividly remember playing on summer break to some sort of soundtrack of the music of the kids just ahead in age; we are passively collecting music at that stage but we also subconsciously make choices and the first album you bought yourself whether tactile or download was a product of that. Music is formative. And just like that, she was back to the magic of college and that drafting of who everyone was trying to be. Or even just who they thought they might like to be.

With time, Thranduil's slightly arrogant affectations had faded, at least when he was with Natalie, Matt and Karla, and he was actually a really good rhythm guitarist, and could play a penny whistle well enough to get by. It made the folk tunes sound so much better and along with the hand drum Karla took to, they sounded pretty darn good. They'd focused on 10 songs, practicing them over and over until they sounded smooth and on occasion, SU staff came and sat in the back and listened.

Sometimes it only looked like staff came in and sat, or at least Nat had thought so but she'd look up a minute after seeing them come in and see nothing. She thought about the talk about hauntings and just smiled. At least they didn't sound as ragged and amateur as they had when they started so if the possible ghost liked music, it wasn't liable to be ashamed of them.

THREE

Despite having said they were just in it for the jam sessions, an opportunity came up to participate in a music event at the other, older theater on campus. around December. Each band was being allotted a block of time and they kicked around a lot of options from among the songs they'd more or less perfected. In the end, they settled on *Twa Sisters, She Moved Through the Fair, James Harris* (also called *The House Carpenter*), *The Wife at Usher's Well*, with several options just in case another band played one of these. The alternates included *The Unquiet Grave* and *Proud Lady Margaret*. Since all but one mentioned ghosts, this brought up the haunted theater thing, of course, again. Karla made a remark about something that sounded very much like the shadow Natalie had seen watching and Thranduil tried to tart it up, but no one wanted to feed his enthusiasm. It was like before when he sounded like he was trying to scare them, but this time Natalie knew him better and thought she could sense that at least half of it was him trying to scare himself. Or talk away the feeling that it was true because he was already spooked. For her own part, Natalie wasn't convinced the theater was haunted. Despite the shadowy shapes that the house lights cast, she didn't think it *felt* haunted. Not the way she'd experienced hauntings before, anyway.

"Every theater is haunted," Karla said dismissively to turn the conversation but not until after Thranduil had told stories about about a friend who worked stage crew and had heard a sound like a bowling ball rolling around on the stage after set strike when the place was empty, with never a good reason to explain it. There had also been the one where there was a coffee pot on a stair landing halfway up the cast area that would turn itself on when no one was in the building, and a green room where someone had legendarily died, leaving a stain on the floor that couldn't be removed (mildew, said Natalie's logical mind. Bad housekeeping and old flooring.) Admittedly, this stage, despite being newer than the other campus venue, really was an old beat-up thing, not glamorous or pretty, at least not anymore, and the old orchestra pit had been filled in years ago, leaving an eerie and rather sad set of stairs embedded in a wall below stage where the dressing rooms were. And there was a radiator on the ceiling in the ladies' room, and a musty old costume storage area that was shaped like a warped wedge and smelled like mold. Old buildings had creepy interest but all this also made the ghost stories seem more real somehow. She wondered if the other theater was going to be any better. Since the older theater differed in everything from outlets to stage size, they had signed up for a rotation to practice in the venue six weeks before the event dates and she hadn't been in it yet but as Karla had just said, every theater was probably haunted. She'd find out next weekend when they began serious practice for the performance.

Matt took her to a party one weekend. Originally, the others were going to be there too, and Joann had been invited, which was nice of him, but Jo had found another circle of friends and had talked about nothing except starting her own band the last few times Natalie had seen her so Natalie had sort of just let that friendship slide. There were other kids she was seeing often now instead of Jo who filled the companionship role within the context of learning, and out of it, and she was pretty sure Jo didn't miss her company either.

This weekend, with just Matt for familiarity, the party was again a bit like jumping off a bridge of the known into a void of the unknown. He had picked her up on his motorcycle because the night was going to be dry, and the ride over to some random house in the sticks was cool and fun. The sun hadn't gone down when they left, and there was a soft yellow haze over the countryside. She was surprised that even when wearing the loaner helmet she could smell flowers on the roadside, and somehow the magic steel steed thing was not lessened by the roar of the engine, the stink of the exhaust that permeated her clothes, or the fact that she had to put her arms around Matt's waist to keep from falling off. She'd been on a bike back once before but this time it seemed different. Probably the daylight fading as the day came to a close helped:  trees stirred gently in the breeze by the time they pulled up to the busy well-lit house in an older neighborhood, and the air carried the voices of party-goers to them from half a block away. She had a distinct Halloween feeling, even though it was November.

Similar to the beer party that first month, it was a mix of kids from all class ranges, and interest groups. The actors were talking about Shakespeare and Natalie, who had declined to drink this round, thought about the music, wondering if they could do an arrangement of the *Willow Song* from Othello, or one of the Macbeth witches' spells set to music but she herself wasn't a writer and so far, the others

had been content to do covers so they probably weren't either. The house the party was held in assisted with the sort of things people were discussing as it had a library absolutely jammed with books of all kinds but also leaning toward the creepy and Victorian mourning side of thing, with a rare example of hair art on the wall, and what looked like a real skull, and things in jars. There were also plastic Halloween decorations so the home-owner was indiscriminately into the spooky. It fit in with everything in Natalie's world these days, from the darkening weather to the music they were

working, and it seemed like it wasn't just them. The world that was this college seemed to be about discovery and fantasy worlds, both of which lent material for figuring out what you liked. Role playing games like Dungeons and Dragons and science fiction books--the original old-school stuff, mostly--along with classic literature from Dumas and Phillip K. Dick to Kotzwinkle and Walter M. Miller all featured highly in the conversations. Tom Robbins had just and *Still Life with Woodpecker* was one of several almost mandatory books for new college students, with Kurt Vonnegut's *Slaughterhouse Five*. She heard people discussing literature and film, mostly foreign films, and others just talking about their concentration, whatever it was. The math corner seemed pretty empty though the two students discussing something about imaginary numbers were passionate (or drunk) enough to be getting heated about it. It was sort of funny, but also typical. People she knew these days seemed to get so *into* things.

The party was a neat moment of something unique. It was dark, details were indistinct, people were brighter and more energetic and probably way more artificial than they would be by broad

daylight. The night made it okay to be somebody more fun. Natalie figured this was exactly why Halloween appealed: you got to be anything you wanted, even if it was only one night. If she was honest with herself, everything for the last five or so years felt like pretend, anyway. She, like her friends, had been trying things and presenting herself in different ways to see who she might become but today, here and now with Matt, she decided she wasn't going to try to put herself in a certain light or say things that would make him think of her in a certain

way. She would just say what she thought, and see what happened.

It seemed to be working, but probably that was because they'd now known each other for many weeks. It was the first time she'd been alone with him more or less, though, and it made her a little nervous. Thankfully, Matt didn't seem to see that, or he didn't care. Like the first party, he didn't seem

like he was apt to treat this as a date, which was more comfortable than if he had. She had to admit to herself that she definitely liked him, liked him, but she would've been mortified if he knew it. Talk about his classes and hers had been desultory, and when they got onto music, much more of interest to both, there was a pause and he said, looking out over the crowd rather than at Natalie,

"Thand wasn't wrong about that theater being spooky. I have heard things, and once or twice I think I've seen things too."

Natalie was flattered to be given this insight but also not sure why, when he'd so thoroughly refused to ever be drawn into such conversations, he did so now.

"Why are you telling me?" It was an honest question, pitched kindly but she wanted to know and having had paranormal encounters in her own life, was curious about his.

Matt shrugged and looked down at her with a faint grin that wasn't about humor as much as curiosity of his own:

"You weren't laughing. When he got on the suicide girl and all that."

Natalie shrugged too and looked away, unsure if she wanted to discuss her own stuff but hey, you told yourself to be real, so risk it. She said,

"I've had things happen to me so I'm the last one to tell you it's bull. And," her voice had a high descending sigh in it, slightly ramped up for effect, "I thought I saw someone listening to us play a few times that couldn't be there but I think it was the way the lights hit the edge of the proscenium." She smiled at him. Matt smiled back,

"You're probably right. Noises and shadows that look like people are nothing to Thranduil's buddy with the bowling balls on stage."

"True. That'd be really freaky."

Talk turned into other channels but Natalie felt like they'd reached a bit of a bond there, over not judging each other about it or trying to make something big and funny or spooky out of it. It just was. The not knowing if it was real or not was fine, and that was enough.

When Natalie arrived home from school the next night, there was a note on the kitchen table, the common spot for communications when she or Peg was apt to miss the other. It said that Peg was out with friends and wouldn't be home until late. Natalie, who had been unable to not notice the basement stairs as she passed them on the way to the inside door of the kitchen, wasn't totally thrilled to be alone again and she was even less happy about it when, while making an early dinner for herself, she heard a tinkle of melody from the basement that sounded like one of the songs she'd been practicing with the band.

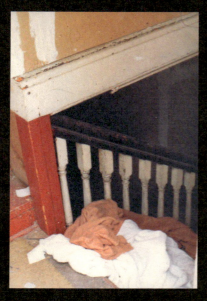

She stopped dead and listened with that heart-pounding, temperature-raising instant panic response that she knew from prior paranormal incidents in her life. The sound did not repeat but she could hear it in her head clearly, the sound of either music or of something breaking in the basement to which she alone had access. And it had definitely resembled a melody. Music box? Glass bottle hitting the floor? But why would it have fallen after months of no one ever going down there? She tried to ignore it and get on with soup and crackers but there was a sort of all-house groan as the building shifted in the cooling wind and it made her jump, made her attention rivet back to the basement even though that wasn't where the latest sound had come from, nor was it unexplained. Still. If she was going to get sleep tonight, she was going to have to go down and look. She didn't want to but she wasn't going to get to it if she didn't do it now. It was still not quite dark out so okay. She'd go downstairs. She'd been around ghosts, and neither had been frightening other than because they had been things of the unknown, so if the person on the stairs was a ghost, it wasn't going to hurt her.

She told herself this again as she found a flashlight and exited the kitchen, leaving all the lights on as she went. The basement light was stupidly placed so that you had to go down into the dark at the bottom of the stairs and halfway across the room to reach it. Since the only thing down there was the furnace and some old lumber and junk no one ever used like a rotted old tin tub and some yard tools, it had never mattered to her before but it sure felt like it mattered now when she'd have to thread through the junk to get to the light switch to see what had just broken. She was thinking all this as she unlocked the inside kitchen door and went down the three stairs to the landing. On the left now as she hesitated was the stairs to the basement. The bottom was in a pool of complete stygian blackness

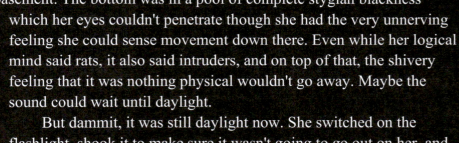

which her eyes couldn't penetrate though she had the very unnerving feeling she could sense movement down there. Even while her logical mind said rats, it also said intruders, and on top of that, the shivery feeling that it was nothing physical wouldn't go away. Maybe the sound could wait until daylight.

But dammit, it was still daylight now. She switched on the flashlight, shook it to make sure it wasn't going to go out on her, and started down the stairs. A lot of junk had been thrown down those stairs by previous tenants or the owners, and no one had picked up the old bedding or broken tools, etc. There was a yard fork abandoned halfway down and she picked it up. She wasn't coordinated or trained enough to make an effective weapon out of it if she needed it, but it made her feel better. A little.

Passing the spot on the stairs that always felt like someone was standing on it made her shiver briefly; it felt like there had been a solid panel of air there that was thicker than the rest but admittedly there had been nothing real to indicate that, no temperature shift, no draft or breeze, and she was through it and on the bare concrete floor in a split second. From there, the flashlight showed her the light switch and she wove around a few bits of junk to it. It came on instantly, to her relief, and she looked around. The furnace hummed to itself competently, and while there was a fair amount of garbage around, the floor itself was swept clean, showing no traces of anything shattered, and no odd materials that might have been able to make the noise she'd heard, like, say, an old piano sounding board or broken ukulele. There also was no other person there and no hints of rats or mice. Satisfied at least that nothing was wrong and thinking she may have heard a sound on the street and mis-directed it mentally, Natalie oriented herself, then switched off the light. For a few seconds, her eyes were too dilated to be able to see anything even with her flashlight. It was like there was a black blanket hanging between her and the foot of the stairs, i.e. the way out. For some reason, that was scarier than anything and she stumbled forward too fast for safety. She did reach the stairs and get halfway up before her eyes adjusted totally and at the top of the flight, made herself turn and look down. The last vestige of retinal burn from the light to dark transition made the darkness at the bottom look like a human shape. Just for a second. She didn't have the courage to face it just now and fled for the safety of the kitchen.

It took her most of dinner to calm down and she spent the half hour obsessing over the idea of someone invisible on the stairs who was really angry, intimidatingly angry, and could now move things or make noises. Her logical mind figured she should just talk to it. Mom had said that the first time Natalie had reported a ghost issue. "Ask her what she wants," Mom had suggested. It was a good plan. But not tonight. Natalie had let herself get too scared tonight. She could deal with it tomorrow and anyway, it was late now, fully dark and time to finish some schoolwork anyway.

FOUR

The next night was their first practice in the new, if historically older, venue and Natalie got there late with her keyboard. She had got lost, campus being so big and there was still so much she hadn't seen yet.

The boys sympathized but Karla was in a mood tonight and said abruptly,

"Let's get started."

Natalie didn't take it personally though she felt a twinge of that little kid with the older kids thing, which she had not felt for ages with this group. She knew Karla was studying on a high level so it was almost certainly sleeplessness and stress that made her crabby. Even if it wasn't, Natalie was going to try to ignore it. She got her gear set up while the guitarists tuned.

Sunset had been orange and dusty blue stripes of clouds shifting toward a bright horizon when she'd come in, and the colors had been festive, which was a good way to start a Friday. The campus was emptying as students and faculty finished classes and began to leave, and the band could hear animated voices laughing and passing the doors and echoing weirdly in the auditorium like whispers. This went on all through set-up but it was eerily quiet before they were ready to go, at least until they started playing. They launched into *Twa Sisters.* After the first verse and chorus, there was a crashing noise from backstage that brought them to a straggling halt.

"What the hell was that?" Matt, irritated, unslung his guitar and put it on the stand.

"Ignore it," Karla said, "It's probably something the last group didn't put away right."

"Go on without me, I'll be right back." Matt disappeared backstage and was gone for half the next song. It sounded thin without his guitar. When he reappeared, it was with a bemused look on. "Nothing I can see," he reported.

Natalie was reminded of her basement last night and suppressed a faint shudder. All theaters are haunted. Right. And this was older than the SU auditorium too. Karla was too worried about getting the practice in before she had to get home and work her butt off over books so she moved them on,

"If it's not leaking and it isn't on fire, it isn't important. Come on, I'm on a schedule."

Nothing else weird happened for the rest of the play, though Natalie was sure she did hear some clanking and bonking noises from behind and under the stage that didn't sound like normal theater sounds but she said nothing. If anyone else noticed, they were ignoring it. It wasn't until after they'd finished and were packing up that Natalie found out there had been a conversation before she

arrived and it had been all about how it was this theater, not the newer auditorium, that was connected to the girl falling off the balcony story. As always, people repeated legend over and over until you couldn't tell who had started it or how much truth it might have, but this seemed to have been a long-standing fable handed down from student to student. And that was part of why Karla had been touchy. Natalie got that: she also now understood why Matt had insisted on a search.

It happened the next session too, and the next. Once the music started each practice, there would be some noise or other, sometimes loud, sometimes more like knocking or footsteps. The second night, Karla joined Matt in the search and the third, they all split up to look, it had been so loud. Natalie and Thranduil had taken the upper floor and balcony but there was no one in the theater portion of the property and the doors were all firmly locked. For a moment, Natalie stood in the corner of the balcony, looking down at the stage where Karla was just coming out from the wings. Below, Matt was a dark shape moving up the aisle from the rear of the house and it was a neat view of what the concert would look like. For a second, Natalie could imagine herself on the stage behind her keyboard, matching harmonies to Karla's strong lead vocals, while the boys bent over their guitars, Matt with his dark head down in absolute focus, and Thranduil with his head thrown back from time to time, executing really beautiful riffs that walked the line between metal and folk. Karla would be in a follow spot. To Natalie's left, the big metal cannon-like spotlight sat dark in a little

thrust of the balcony, waiting. For a second, it had looked like a person was standing behind it but as she looked right at it, it was just shadows from the stage lights casting an impression into the corner. She had to get on top of her nerves. It wasn't like this would be her first paranormal experience and anyway, wasn't it supposed to be SU with the ghost, not this? At least she hadn't heard anything. Yet. She sighed and went back to the stairs that took them down to the main floor, reminding herself that even if it was haunted, ghosts almost never actually hurt people. Which only helped some.

The next few nights were repeats of the program, these starting with a search of the building before they commenced practice. They alternated search zones so Natalie got to see the backstage, the wings, the projection booth. Each night, there was no one but themselves in the building, and the doors were locked but the noises still came and they sounded less and less natural and more and more human. After a while, even Natalie, ghost-experienced, was beginning to wish it would stop. Two days before the show, there was a huge storm and after a practice full of knockings and footsteps, she lay awake in her haunted rental listening to the voice of the wind around the house corners, and the sound of the house creaking and ticking to itself. She couldn't separate the sound of, say, the kitchen vent, or the upside-down transom window in the bathroom from the sound of the door to the basement so it was a rough night and school the next day was a real chore.

It never happened by daylight, however. On the day before the gig, Natalie and crew were in the auditorium helping set up backdrops along with various other band members who were to perform at the festival and all of which had been tapped to act as stage crew since the original program for stage craft had been scrapped by officious school staff who somehow thought it was more cost-effective to use volunteer stage hands than train up the next generation of professionals. As a result. there were probably 20 amateur stage crew muddling around getting things done and sometimes not getting things done the confusion of which was added to when, without editorial noises but in mysterious silence, tools would go missing regularly but turn up in odd places (a box wrench for the risers was set down by someone's knee and vanished, to be found 10 minutes later beneath the fly rail. No one would admit to having moved it.) There were too many people milling around to tell whether or not the atmosphere included a person no one could see but toward evening, there began to be clunking noises from backstage when everyone was in the house and accounted for, and the building sighed now and then, which was unnerving. Natalie, thinking of the house in the storm and acutely aware that the weather tonight was virtually windless and clear, caught Matt's eye once just after a really obvious sigh and he dropped his own quickly with a chin jerked sideways. Karla saw it and said blandly,

"The wind sure howls around the roof in here, doesn't it?" But her eyes were a little too wide and alert. Thranduil said nothing but every single time a noise occurred that could possibly be put down to the invisible, he looked at his bandmates. Around them, other people made blithe comments and complaints about stages and theaters and one made a ghost crack, which was interesting because it implied they'd heard stuff too when practicing alone in the last weeks. No one quite had the nerve to ask outright though, so no information was forthcoming about the old place, or possible inhabitants no one could see.

The afternoon was golden and brisk but the night before the gig had turned cold again and gotten blustery, which at least had the advantage of blurring the unaccountable noises from the building. This was the last chance to practice in the space before they'd be doing it for an audience, and Natalie's group, who were calling themselves Child's Children for lack of anything better, were last up. As they tuned, Natalie was aware of a feeling of nervousness, blame her active imagination that was peopling the seats with a crowd. It wasn't until halfway through the first song that the feeling of anxiety shifted. It became less about potential watchers than about a potential *watcher,* and she gradually noticed that the part of her attention not focused on the music was watching something back out of the corner of her eye. It wasn't there when she looked straight out into the seats but when she had her head turned, it seemed like there was a solid black person-shape in the middle seats. The lights, set for tomorrow, of course made it really hard to see into the house but the impression was still pretty obvious that close to the stage. When the song ended, she looked around at her bandmates and was about to say something when the first of the loud noises came.

The other bands and the stage manager had long since filtered away, taking the bustle of excited performers and fretting organizers with them, so the sound had more impact than it might have, had there been someone left in the theater besides Matt, Karla, Thranduil and Natalie. Matt, distracted with a retune, said idly,

"Someone still backstage?"
Karla glanced around, distracted herself by a crappy mic-stand,
"Should be just us now." She didn't point out that they'd already checked the entire building in their by-now swift and well-practiced pre-practice search.
Clonk. Rustle.

"Too loud for rats," Thranduil said it almost like he hadn't meant to speak out loud. He looked at Natalie, who shrugged as a sound like something toppling over came, farther back but still clearly backstage. She said,

"Do we want to go looking?" She didn't say "again" but she thought it. At this point, the idea of ghosts had been pretty much associated in her mind with this band no matter where they practiced, and of her rental situation, but even though it unnerved her, and the home front made her really, really nervous, so far nothing had really done anything but scare her. Logically, and by experience, she had no reason to think anything could happen that could do anything but frighten.

Clonk. Rustle, rustle, click. Possible backstage footsteps. A sound of something hitting the grid thirty feet overhead.

Matt, head up and listening hard, finally said,

"Yeah." He didn't move at once though and the sound of someone walking behind the flats was clear to all. "Yeah."

Matt signed heavily then led off, unslinging his guitar and putting it on the stand while in motion, like he was going to go yell at some kid who was making noise while they were trying to play but Natalie could see his shoulders were too high and his step was reluctant even while it was purposeful. They split up again, Matt and Karla handling backstage which had a crossover space and deep wings with some side rooms. Natalie and Thranduil went up.

It was the first time she'd really noticed the architecture that was the domain of stage technicians here, and she was impressed by how unsafe it seemed. The fly rail off to the left had the traditional belaying pins, and looked just like a sailing ship rail, but half the locks didn't seem to be engaged. Then the grid, from which more distant faint noises were trickling down, was reached by a metal ladder bolted to the concrete back wall of the building. The ladder looked ancient and it seemed to almost vanish from sight when she looked up. Thirty feet had never looked so high before. Clunk, rustle. Thranduil sighed. He had probably been thinking the same thing. He said,

"I'm not good with heights."

Natalie, sensitive to tone via younger siblings, took this to mean he was afraid of heights and didn't want to climb. She looked at his face and saw he looked white in the dim harsh backstage illumination. She felt a little bad because she didn't want to climb that ladder either, but heights didn't

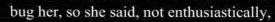

bug her, so she said, not enthusiastically,

"I'll do it."

"Are you sure?"

"Sure. It'll be fun." Her tone said anything but, however, she started up, keeping her eyes ahead and really, the only dodgy part was the top where the ladder ended in a sort of swimming-pool loop only a few feet above the level of the wooden grid. She had to hold onto the top of the ladder by stooping while making the transfer to the wood, which didn't appear to have rails near enough to reach. It was not a comfortable transfer but she made it and stood looking at the maze of wires and wood that constituted a theater grid. Between the slats, she could see the light battens, rigging trusses, the catwalk and the mess of par cans and ellipsoidal lights pointed in all directions. On the grid itself other than hoists and belaying wires, there was mostly just dust and a few buckets. She made her way to the buckets thinking dripping water from the leaky roof might have made the noise but they were all empty and dry. Nothing moved except herself, and no noises came. From up here. Below, on the vacant stage, the same sort of clunky sounds issued and she sighed. To no one she said,

"Thanks for nothing," and carefully climbed back down.

The band found nothing to account for the noises of course which annoyed Natalie though Thranduil and Karla had started kicking around artificially casual remarks that danced around the idea of hauntings.

"We're only spooking ourselves because we're singing ghost songs," Matt said. He didn't sound convinced. Natalie said quietly,

"It's just noise."

Karla shrugged, a sort of abrupt jerk. saying,

"That men's dressing room felt really wrong."

Thranduil opened his mouth to say something but didn't have a chance before a renewed and particularly loud crash came. Karla said flatly,

"That's it. This is freaking me out."

Natalie sounded calm and repeated,

"It's just noise."

"It sounds like a person." This was Thranduil, also flatly.

"Someone who doesn't like this song, or our version," added Karla wryly. Matt had begun running rifts on the next song behind the nervous discussion about paranormal activity.

Natalie laughed and said out loud, spreading the music sheets out on her keyboard,

"Okay, so if you hate *Twa Sisters*, pick another we can play." She took her hands away from

the pages and almost instantly, one drifted onto the stage decking. It would've been nothing unusual except that it wasn't one of the pages on the top or edges, but one from the middle. The other three stared at it with big eyes. Thranduil said,

"What. The. Hell."

Natalie rose and picked up the sheet. It was *The Unquiet Grave*. She turned her voice over her shoulder to address the backstage area and said in a normal tone,

"Is this one a yes or a no?"

An isolated clunk that was distant but clear seemed to answer. She shrugged and took the page back to her keyboard stand.

"Let's do *Unquiet Grave*."

Her bandmates stared at her for a long moment. She eventually realized and looked up,

"What?" She was wondering if the choice was too on-point but didn't say it out loud.

Another long pause stretched as both tried to put words to what they were thinking. Eventually, Thranduil said

"That was freaky."

"Who are you talking to?" said Karla. Her expression was a cross between accusation and a sort of nervously impressed awe.

Natalie shrugged again,

"Anyone who's listening. Try this song and see if the noises stop." And at more staring, "What can it hurt?" Karla shrugged and turned back to her mic but she looked too wide-eyed to signify comfort. Thranduil was just openly staring, his mouth slightly ajar. Matt, though. Matt was looking at her from a shadow between house lights and his face was all in the black except his eyes. He was watching her steadily, just oddly enough that she wished she could see the rest of his face. "Give it a try, anyway," she said, trying to decrease the level of bizarre and almost funny creepiness that seemed to be filling the stage.

No one had an answer to that but Matt started the guitar intro to Child ballad #78. Interestingly, no noises occurred unless the very faint, almost imperceptible feeling of the stage resonating in time to the song was something other than coincidence. It felt like someone was tapping their foot, though no other of their pieces had produced that effect. But old buildings had quirks and all buildings had resonances that could be discovered if someone had enough time or the luck to find them so they ignored it and played. It was the best practice they'd had to date. It was also the first time Natalie felt like they had a real audience member who was paying attention and enjoying themselves.

There was a frosted blur of crescent moon when she got home that night and the wind had fallen again, leaving the night cold but not icy. Thinking of that interaction, or at least that perceived interaction from the perceived ghost of the old theater, Natalie turned the logic toward the rental basement and its unnerving presence. Maybe the stair thing here was only hostile because it was alone. Or, and here was a thought, what if it was a former home-owner? How would Natalie feel if she'd built a house, lived in it her whole life and raised kids there, then had it taken away and inhabited, and damaged, by a succession of adolescent renters who didn't take care of things, or give a damn, or stay. And those people had taken over the living spaces, so the former owner was driven to hide in the basement.

The magic of the music had buoyed her so with a sense of benevolence, she unlocked the door and sat down on the top step beside the old bedding.

"Hi,' she said. "I'm Natalie. I have nothing against you. Neither does Peg, the girl in the front room. We do our best to take care of this place while we're here so please don't bother us. If you want, though, you can come up into the kitchen."

The inside door opened and Peg looked out, initial consternation on her face giving way to bewilderment. She said,

"I thought we had trespassers. Who are you talking to?"

Natalie explained.

"I always get the feeling there's something on the stairs watching me so I decided to talk to it and see if anything happens."

"Huh."

"Haven't you ever noticed?"

"I use the front door." Peg paused, then showing she wasn't totally oblivious to her housemate's moods, said, "Want to switch keys?"

Natalie agreed but had a feeling things wouldn't be so creepy going forward and stood to get her key ring out of her jeans, saying,

"Just be sure to say hi when you come in."

FIVE

The gig was on a weekend so it was going to be well attended, and the weather was agreeing for a change. As bands began to arrive at the venue, the day was closing and allowing a bright brisk night to enter, with excitement and nervousness, and dusk reflected in the puddles of yesterday's rain showers. Light was shifting into darkness in the best of ways.

Load-in was only their portable gear as they were using the house amps, and in the back parking lot which had most of the lights out, the light was failing so fast that colors and shapes were becoming dim and difficult to make out, though the sky still had that deep cobalt blue tone of a truly clear night. After the stormy days, it was refreshing. The buzz of the cast and crew arriving at the theater in a well-washed dusk with a colorful sky was like a party in a way, but with an additional open-door feeling of a large group of people about to conjure up something magic. It was about half theater and half coven on the heath, but Natalie was enjoying the high energy despite a slight memory in back of her head that there was a test on Monday she hadn't studied for very thoroughly. It could wait.

Matt and Karla had come in her crappy red car, while Natalie and Thranduil had each walked. In a tarmac shadow with other bands unloading vehicles and chattering, the four convened with gear in hand.

"Are we ready?" Matt said it. He was in complete darkness with the street light behind him but a white flash implied he was grinning. Karla, in a half light, was smiling for sure and she said,

"Hell yes. Break a leg, people."

Natalie knew that was a traditional theater remark but it always had struck her as encouraging negative things. She said with deliberate lightness,

"Just don't mention the M play." Another bit of theater lore was to never mention the name of Shakespeare's grim historical while undertaking any kind of theatrical performance.

"Never," Thranduil assured her. "Okay? Let's go be nervous while we wait for everyone else to finish, yeah?"

Laughter, a little tight because Natalie *was* nervous. The others seemed more alert and electric than nervous and Matt said,

"So we're not doing *Twa Sisters*, remember. We'll do *Unquiet Grave* instead."

"Like we could forget," Karla said sourly, but with energy. She was looking forward to the show.

"Right. Onward."

The gig went well. All the bands played up to an appreciative audience, though there was a fair amount of coming and going during performances because it was a long show, and more than likely, a large portion of the audience was only present to support friends or family. It didn't matter. Those that stayed seemed to enjoy the work and the content, and Child's Children got a gratifying round of applause even though they were last on stage and the crowd was thinner than it had been. It was also pretty late and people had parties to go to and homework to finish. Natalie didn't mind: she was jazzed by the energy of performance adrenalin and could see her bandmates were too. They hadn't made any overt or major errors and Joann's band, which had also performed, had been in a completely different musical style so there hadn't been any feeling of competition, which Natalie, though she didn't hang out with Jo anymore, was glad of.

She bid goodnight to Matt and Karla, and this time, because it was so late, Thranduil walked

her home. It wasn't unappreciated; the area around campus was pretty safe as towns went but no place with any size population was 100% safe and it was close on midnight. Tonight, Thranduil had his guitar over his back instead of his short sword, but it had a similar effect. Natalie, shielded by darkness and the lingering of a successful show, started a conversation about Fellowship of the Ring. Thranduil was never loathe to discuss his favorite book series, so the walk passed in companionable comfort with the happy spark of shared interests. He also showed her a different way to get from campus to her part of town that went through a wooded area, which during the day would be beautiful but at night she was not going to try alone: the wooded grounds around here were dense with old growth forest remnants and aside from feeling risky for a single girl at night, had a definite vibe of the magical. No wonder Thrand liked it. He talked about the Fangorn when they were in the thickest section and Natalie could feel the black trunks and high branches pause against the sky to listen to his words. There was something about being on a high spot with the original clothing of the land and a man who was something of a knight. The past felt closer and more real. Also swords and sorcery felt closer and more real.

When they reached her house, Thranduil stopped on the sidewalk rather than take her right to the door. She at first assumed it was just because he wasn't trying to smother her with outdated courtesy or date her but when she looked up at his face to say good night, saw he was looking at the house pensively and steadily.

"What?" She was thinking he'd been here before or it reminded him of something. His answer took her off guard:

"Is it haunted?"

Natalie paused a second in surprise tinged with a bit of shock: could he tell from out here? She looked where he was looking, wondering. There wasn't anything special about the place that she could see that would say that. Oh well,

"Yeah. Like everything else around here, I guess."

Thranduil grinned, saying,

"Everything is haunted at the closing of the day. Good night."

SIX

The week after the gig, Matt showed up at the rental on his motorcycle with the spare helmet. They hadn't had any plans so Natalie, mid-homework, came out at Peg's insistence to see who it was honking now and then.

"Hi, is something wrong?" He'd left the motor running.

"Have you got time to go see something?"

"What? I guess so. What is it?"

"I've been doing research." His tone was leading. Natalie, looking at his face betray nothing, nodded,

"Let me get my coat."

He took her to the oldest cemetery in town. The weather consisted of bright sunlight breaking through shifting cloud work and sometimes spitting rain, making the colors gem-like when the sun got the upper hand and hit the landscape with gold. The wind was in the trees, making them shift and spill drops of moisture, and loosening the scent of conifer, grass and dirt. The natural scents blended with the gasoline fumes on

their clothes and the leather of Matt's jacket which was slightly tinged with the cologne he'd worn to the gig a week past. It was quiet despite a road running just past and the freeway not far distant but the place felt wide awake and thronged with people. It wasn't isolated, like most cemeteries. It didn't have that usual envelope of the past, with no active energies. Somehow this one felt like a downtown street, calm, but not empty, quiet but not unaware.

Matt took her to a section that wasn't the oldest but had the sort of monuments popular in the 1960s.

"Look for Karen Louise Guilde, with an e on the end," he said.

Natalie guessed,

"The old theater girl? She was real?"

Matt just nodded, scanning stones. He found it first and they stood looking at the simple flat marker.

"She *was* my age," Natalie remarked. It was sad. It was also the first time she'd had a ghost story confirmed so materially. "Her poor parents."

Matt nodded again.

"I wish I'd thought to bring flowers."

Natalie dug out some change and found three pennies.

"Here."

They laid the coins on the headstone then stood a moment longer looking at the end of a short life. It was sad and somehow, seeing the name engraved there gave the girl who had been just myth a reality she hadn't had before, when she'd been a legend repeated to scare new kids.

On the way out, she said,

"Thanks for bringing me here. I'm amazed you were able to find out who the legend was about."

Matt grunted a sort of laugh,

"I'm amazed it turned out to be true. I couldn't find anything on the SU theater though I did find plenty of reports of people saying they were sure it was haunted."

Natalie repeated what she'd said to Thranduil after the show:

"Seems like everywhere I've been around here is haunted. "

Matt grinned faintly and said to the distance,

"It's an old town. You should see the streets that used to be the red-light district."

On the way home, he drove her past a handful of other spots in the area that were said to be haunted. He told her he'd run across them all while doing the research to find out the origin of the theater story and suggested they do a ghost tour someday, reiterating that the old red-light district by the waterfront was said to be really active. Again, Natalie didn't think it was a date sort of suggestion but she was glad to have the connection and agreed.

"But after mid-terms." Then, "I didn't know you were so interested in ghost stories. Or ghosts or whatever." She blushed, feeling like that might have been pushy.

Matt shrugged,

"I don't talk about it, that's all." There was a tiny hesitation, then, "I saw one when I was a kid. So yeah, interesting."

Natalie nodded.

"Me too."

"Okay," Matt said, like a confirmation.

"Okay," she smiled.

End

PHOTOS
(By Marcia Lins unless otherwise noted)

COVERS:
Fort Worden trail 2018
Backstage by anthony-limmncNxC on unsplash.com

1993 old pier parts Bellingham Bay
Branches, Fremont 2011
Keg by Alberto Biondi on jnsplash.com
Puff balls and hydrangea by Tess, Ferndale 2011
Hotel Boheme clip from internet
Pierris berries Fremont 2007
Chardin Hall. Seattle University 2023
Crop from set by sj-lkw17GKswts on unsplash.com
Spot on stage by Justin Bautista on unsplash.com
Leaf shadows on concrete block by lik-hong on unsplash.com
Black and white Fremont hill c. 1999
Red car by Anton Holmgren on unsplash.com
Stairs and lamp/chair legs at 322 N. Forest 1988
Brick walkway by leiada-krozjhen on unsplash.com
Cobble from Mitchel-lensink (man) and ethan-yoo (walkway) unsplash.com
Cell phone shot 2025
Asia culture center by OtUtCmkEzdU on unsplash.
Rainy concrete by Jack Baxter on unsplash.com
Capitol Hill rainy night c. 1987
322 N. Stairs 1988
Bellingham pier 1993
Dark auditorium by krish-shaw on unsplash,com (edited)
Blue behind the scenes by drew-walker on unsplash.com
Old orchestra pit at Highline High School by Jonathan Nelson 1988
Radiator on the ceiling, Highline basement by Teresa Csorba c. 1985
Costume storage at Highline High School by Jonathan Nelson 1988
The Guide Meridian c. 1994
Clip of a New Orleans party 1999
Steven Bard's House 2008 two shots
Howl O'Scream Williamsburg crop 2008

322 N. Forest stairs 1988

Dark stairs by jeremie-crausaz on unsplash.com

Red seats by kevin-schmid (cropped) on unsplash.com

Sunset at Bill's House 2006

Projection booth at Old Highline High School by Jonathan Nelson 1988

3232 N. Forest bathroom 1988

Freeway up to Bellingham 2012

Karen-zhao red theater on unsplash.com (adjusted)

Crop of the breakers at Mt. Baker theater c.1990

Ladder byli-lin on unsplash.com (cropped)

View from the grid off internet

Dressing room at Highline High School by Jonathan Nelson 1988

Sheet music by sarah-dao on unsplash.com

Moon by cheolmin-kin on unsplash.com (edited)

Porch light at 322.N. Forest 1988

Keyboard by Gerold-hinzen on unsplash.com

Guitarist by sam-vanagtmael on unsplash.com

Mic by BjoernEngelke on unsplash.com

Woods by florian-weichert on unsplash.com

322 N. Forest by Teresa Csorba in infrared 2011

Two shots of Bayview Cemetery 2009

Hill Crest Cemetery, Bainbridge Island 2024

Pennies from Lakeview graves 2009

Bellingham Armory by Teresa Csorba 2011

Accents:

Foggy rest at Smokey Point c.2013

Fields near Bellingham c.2015

Smokey Point again

Mount Baker Theater dome

Mount Baker forest 1986

322 N. Forest kitchen window 1987

Lit branches, Capitol Hill 2025

Clouds on blue Flagler Thanksgiving 2023

Basement room HIghline High School by Jonathan Nelson 1988

Bayview cemetery angel, Bellingham 2009

Tin whistle 2025

Steve Bard's library 2008

SPU Campion Hall 2023

Sunset in NP 2024

No persons in this story are meant to portray anyone living or dead. While I happen to know a Natalie who is going to college right now (my alma mater, no less), she is not in any way connected to this character, who was named at random some years ago. My apologies if that is a problem the the real girl, and also, go Corndogs!